MUCH ADO
ABOUT JULIET

DISNEY PRESS

New York

DISNEY
MINNIE & DAISY
BEST FRIENDS FOREVER

best friends

For more information address Disney Press,
114 Fifth Avenue, New York, New York 10011-5690.

ISBN 978-1-4231-7268-0

J689-1817-1-13060
Printed in the United States of America

First Edition

10 9 8 7 6 5 4 3 2 1

For more Disney Press fun, visit disneybooks.com

SUSTAINABLE
FORESTRY
INITIATIVE

Certified Chain of Custody
Promoting Sustainable Forestry

www.sfiprogram.org
SFI-01415
The SFI label applies to the text stock.

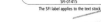

Chapter 1

"**D**aisy! Did you hear? They're putting on a school play!"

Minnie Mouse ran up to her best friend, Daisy Duck. As usual, Daisy was walking fast through the halls of Mouston Central School. Daisy was always on the move. It was one of the things Minnie loved about her.

"Mornin', Min," Daisy said, smiling at her friend.

Minnie smiled back. She was still practically hopping up and down with excitement. "So," Minnie said, "did you hear what the play is?"

"Romeo and Juliet, right?"

Daisy said. "**Lame.**"

"But it's so . . . so . . . *romantic!*" Minnie said. "Shakespeare's *Romeo and Juliet* is the greatest love story of all time!"

"Ugh," Daisy said. "I'm sure it's a wonderful story. But every school play is always the same. That drama nut Paul Poser gets the lead part. All the other roles go to his drama groupies and the

popular kids like Abigail.
Lame!"

"I guess . . . " Minnie
said. She knew what Daisy
meant. But still . . . "Paul
isn't so bad, you know,"
Minnie said.

"All he thinks about is
acting!" Daisy said. "And
every girl in this school
thinks he's **soooooo
dreamy**."

Minnie was starting to feel a little annoyed
with her friend. Daisy had strong opinions. But
she didn't always stop to think about how other
people felt.

"Just because he isn't into sports doesn't
mean he isn't cool," Minnie said. The truth was,
she was one of the girls who thought Paul was
"sooooo dreamy." Just thinking about him made
Minnie's heart go bump-a-bump. Oh, Paul! His

big brown eyes . . . his soft brown hair . . .

"That's why I signed up to audition," Minnie said. **"If they cast me as Juliet, I get to kiss Paul Poser!"**

Daisy rolled her eyes. "Seriously?" she said.

"Seriously," Minnie replied. She hated disagreeing with her friend. But Daisy was just wrong about Paul! Paul was sensitive and creative and talented.

"All Paul cares about is Paul," Daisy said.

"You're just going to make it worse by falling all over him."

"Well, I don't care," Minnie said stubbornly. She had a giant crush on Paul, and Daisy was just going to have to deal with it.

"You're crazy, Min," Daisy said. But she was smiling. Minnie smiled back.

"I don't know what you see in these artistic types," Daisy said. "Give me a jock any day. But you're not me, you're you. If you like this guy so much, I'll help you with the audition."

"Daisy, you're the best!" Minnie squealed. She hugged her friend tight.

"Oof!" Daisy said. Minnie's hug had knocked all the air out of her. "Well, what are friends for, right?"

"What are *BFFs* for, you mean!" Minnie said.

"You betcha, BFF," Daisy said, grinning. "Now, sign here."

Daisy pointed to the audition sign-up sheet that was taped up next to the drama classroom door. Minnie wrote her name carefully. Her dream of kissing Paul Poser was finally going to come true!

Chapter 2

Minnie could hardly sit still during her morning classes. She doodled pictures of Paul on her math work sheet. She read *Romeo and Juliet* instead of "Know Your Sloths" in science class.

Finally, it was time for lunch. Minnie hurried to the cafeteria. But before she could tell Daisy about her ideas for the audition . . .

"Excuse me," someone sneered. Minnie turned around. There was Abigail, the snobbiest queen bee in the entire school.

"Ex*cuse* her," said **Millie** and **Molly**, Abigail's two-girl fan club. They followed her everywhere.

"I saw your name on the sign-up sheet for the play," Abigail said. "And I hate to burst your bubble, but my *mother* is a *famous actress*. That means *I* will be playing Juliet. *Not you*." She poked Minnie right in the chest. Hard.

"Why, I—" Minnie said angrily. Minnie was so mad she couldn't even finish a sentence. Luckily, Daisy didn't have that problem.

"That's pretty sad, Abigail," Daisy said. "You must be a terrible actress."

"I am not!" Abigail said.

"Sure you are," Daisy said. "You just said it yourself. The only reason for you to get the part is because of your mother."

Abigail looked annoyed. "Whatever. At least I can speak in full sentences," she said. Then Abigail turned to Minnie. "How are you going to play Juliet if you can't even stick up for yourself?" she said in a nasty voice. "Is Daisy going to do your audition for you, too?" She cackled like a witch, and, of course, her little followers joined in. "Bye-bye, losers," Abigail said to Minnie and Daisy. She put her nose in the air and marched off.

"Don't worry," Daisy told Minnie. She sat down at a table and patted the chair next to her. "Abigail is nothing but a bully. She's the loser, not you."

"She said we were *both* losers," Minnie pointed out. She sat down and unpacked her lunch.

"Then you know she's wrong, because **I am awesome**," Daisy said with a grin. Minnie smiled back, weakly. She knew Daisy was trying to cheer her up. But Minnie had a big knot in her stomach.

"Listen," Daisy said after lunch. "Don't let that loudmouth snob get you down."

"But I've never auditioned for anything," Minnie replied.

Daisy winked at Minnie. "You've got me in

your corner. We'll practice your audition until
you know Juliet's part forward and backward."

"Really?" Minnie was surprised. She
knew Daisy thought the whole thing was dumb.

"I owe you," Daisy said. "Remember last
year when you sewed up the tear in my tennis
skirt? You saved my tail feather. Literally. Now
it's my turn to save yours. I'll meet you after
school and we can get started."

Chapter 3

When the school day was over, Daisy met Minnie at her locker. Minnie pulled out a beautiful princess dress.

"See?" Minnie said. "I've been hard at work. I spent every afternoon last week in the library! I was reading about making costumes."

"Wow," Daisy said. Her eyes widened. "You *made* this?"

"Yeah!" Minnie said happily. "Look, the sleeves are made of silk, and the rest is satin. I even made a lace petticoat so the skirt would be

nice and poofy!"

"**Wow,**" Daisy said, shaking her head.

You've got real talent, Minnie!"

"Well," Minnie said, feeling a little shy, "talent only gets you so far."

She held out the dress so Daisy could see it better. Something small and gold flashed from the shoulder. Daisy leaned closer.

"Is that . . . ?" Daisy started to ask.

"Yep!" Minnie said. She smiled at Daisy. "It's my BFF pin. Last night I sewed it on the dress for good luck!"

Daisy grinned. "I'm sure it will work," she said. "Remember when I had my big soccer game last spring?"

"You wore your BFF pin on your soccer jersey!" Minnie said.

"And remember what happened? My team won, *and* my crush asked me out!" Daisy said. "Trust me, the pins work. So when do we start practicing your lines?"

"I've got my piano lesson tonight," Minnie said. "How about tomorrow night?"

"Sure thing, Beethoven," Daisy said. "Or should I call you Shakespeare now?"

"How about sticking to Minnie?" Minnie said. "That's my *name*, after all."

"Okeydokey Captain Obvious!" Daisy said. She ran off before Minnie could pinch her.

Chapter 4

Ding-dong! Minnie heard the door bell ring. Full of excitement, Minnie ran to the door and pulled it open.

"Ready to get dramatic?" Daisy asked. She was still wearing her tennis clothes. There was a tennis racquet tucked under her arm.

Minnie pointed at the tennis racquet. "Did you win?" she asked.

"Duh!" Daisy said. "I am the tennis *queen*."

"Come in, Your Highness," Minnie said. "Let's practice the ball scene."

The two friends settled down in Minnie's room. Minnie handed Daisy a copy of *Romeo and Juliet*.

"Wait," Daisy said, "it says here my part is the nurse."

"You're Juliet's babysitter," Minnie explained.

"I should be *your* babysitter," Daisy said. "You need someone watching out for you so you don't walk into a wall every time Paul Poser walks by!"

"I'm pretty sure that's what BFFs do, not babysitters," Minnie said, poking Daisy. "So I'm all set."

"You really like Paul, huh?" Daisy said.

"I really, really do," Minnie answered. "And if I get the role of Juliet, maybe Paul will ask me out!"

"Oh, now I get it," Daisy said. She grinned wickedly and threw a pillow at Minnie's head. "You're auditioning for the role of Paul Poser's **girrrrlfriennnnd.**"

Daisy clasped her hands. She put a moony look on her face. She batted her eyelashes. "Pauleo, oh, Pauleo!" she said in a high, silly voice. "Why art thou so dreamy, Pauleo?"

*✳

Minnie couldn't help but laugh at Daisy. "Okay, fine!" she said. "But even you have to admit he's really cute."

"I guess," Daisy said. "He's sort of a Justin Beakber type. All serious and sensitive, right?"

"Exactly!" Minnie said. She was glad Daisy could see it her way. "He's so *fascinating*. So . . . *intense*."

"Well," Daisy said, "Paul seems to think so, too. But if anyone could get his attention, Min, it's you."

The two friends practiced Minnie's audition scene for the rest of the evening. Finally, Daisy had to go home.

"I've got tennis practice tomorrow," Daisy said, "so I won't be able to come watch you audition. But I know you'll do great!"

Minnie hugged her friend.

"Fingers crossed," Daisy said.

"Fingers crossed," Minnie agreed.

aisy spent the next day thinking about two things: Minnie's audition and tennis. Lately, Daisy had been working on how she held her tennis racquet.

"Any ideas about the tennis grip?" Daisy's social studies teacher asked the class. Daisy's **hand shot into the air.**

"It's all in the wrist!" Daisy said.

"I said, 'Any ideas about the *class trip*,' Daisy," the teacher said. The class giggled.

After her classes were over, Daisy stopped by

Minnie's locker to wish her luck.

"Miss Mouse!" an angry voice
yelled. Daisy and Minnie whirled around. It was the
vice principal! He frowned at Minnie. Daisy was
surprised. Usually she was the one in trouble,
not Minnie!

"Are you the **troublemaker** who took
out all the books on costume design?" the vice

principal said. Daisy hid a smile behind her hand. Guilty as charged, Minnie, she thought.

"The librarian says they are all overdue!" the vice principal said. "Your punishment is: you must spend the afternoon in the library, shelving books."

"But Mister Vice Principal!" Minnie cried, "I have to audition for the role of Juliet today!"

"I happen to know auditions don't start until four," the vice principal replied. "That gives you an hour to work in the library. **You will pay for your library crimes,** Minnie Mouse, or I am not the vice principal of Mouston Central School!"

ennis practice was a bust. Daisy played her best game, but nobody else did. Everyone on the tennis team was obsessed with the school play! They were all too distracted to think about tennis.

"Who do you think will play Romeo?" one girl said.

"Paul Poser, *of course*," said another.

"Hello?!" Daisy said, throwing a tennis ball at the group of girls. "Is anyone actually playing tennis here?"

"I hear they're building a big set for the play," the tennis coach said. "With a balcony and everything!"

"Those dummies better get their act together," Daisy said to herself as she went back

to her locker after practice. "The **big match** against Glomgold Preparatory School is next week. And they creamed us last year!"

Daisy always tried her hardest at sports. She hated it when other people didn't even make an effort. And she really, really wanted her team to win next week! Daisy loved winning. She loved the spotlight.

"I'll be *so mad* if this stupid play costs us the match," Daisy grumbled. *"So. Mad."*

Just then, Daisy's foot hit something on the floor. *Clink!* She looked down.

It was Minnie's BFF pin! She and Minnie had bought the two matching pins from an old fortune-teller at a flea market.

"These are true friendship hearts," the fortune-teller had told them. "Keep them safe and you'll both have good luck." And they had.

But now Minnie was walking into her first big

audition . . . without her lucky pin!

"Oh, *tail feathers!*" Daisy said. She had to get the pin to Minnie right away! Daisy slammed her locker door shut and took off at a dead sprint. "Heads up! Outta my way! Watch it!" Daisy yelled at anyone in her path.

Was it possible that Minnie hadn't had her audition yet? Daisy hoped so. She knew a whole lot of kids were trying out for the play. She only hoped that Minnie was at the end of the line.

"I'm coming, Minnie!" Daisy said.

Chapter 7

Daisy skidded into the backstage area. There were students in costume everywhere.

"Have you seen Minnie?" Daisy said to her friend Leonard, a tall kid with red hair.

"'To be, or not to be?'" Leonard replied. "'That is the question.'"

"No help there," Daisy muttered to herself. "How about you guys?" she asked the other students.

"'Fie, my lord, fie!'" said a girl wearing a ghost costume.

"'This fellow is wise enough to play a fool,'" said a girl in bloomers.

"You're all fools, as far as I'm concerned," Daisy said crossly. *Where is Minnie?*

"*Alack!*" cried a voice in alarm. Daisy's head whipped around. But Minnie was nowhere to be seen—it was just Paul Poser. He was on the stage, bossing around the spotlight operator.

"'*Swounds*, Mike!" Paul said to the student working the spotlight. "Move the light! *Forsooth*, it flatters not my hairstyle!"

"Paul is already in character, I see . . ." Daisy muttered to herself. "As a jerk!"

But what was that? A familiar hair bow peeked out from behind a pile of props on the other side of the stage. It was Minnie!

Daisy bolted across the stage, running right by Paul Poser.

"I beg your pardon!" Paul said as Daisy pushed by him.

"It's an emergency,"

Daisy said. Paul looked confused. "Alack," Daisy translated. "My fairest friend hath lost her pin of friendship and good fortune. I must needs return it to her!"

"I understand," Paul said.

Daisy was running at top speed when she reached Minnie.

Crash! Daisy tumbled into Minnie, holding up the BFF pin as they collided.

"Oof!" Minnie said. "Daisy, what—?"

"Did you audition yet?" Daisy asked, interrupting her.

"**N-n-n-no!**" Minnie said, her head wobbling back and forth.

"**Great geese in garters!**" Daisy said. "That was close!" She let out a long breath. She'd made it to Minnie in time!

"What was close?" Minnie asked from the ground.

"Min, your BFF pin fell off your dress!" Daisy said. She pointed at the shoulder of Minnie's beautiful gown.

"Oh, no!" Minnie said. "That would have been—"

"A disaster! I know!" Daisy agreed. "So I ran all the way here!"

"Such **drama!**" said a voice behind them. Daisy turned. Paul Poser and Mrs. Drake, the drama teacher, were watching them. "Such **action!**" Paul said. **"She's a natural."**

Chapter 8

"**I** know!" Daisy said to Paul. "Minnie is great—"

"Not her," Paul replied, interrupting her. He pointed right at Daisy. "*You.*"

"Me?" Daisy said.

"Her?" Minnie said. Daisy helped her up off the floor.

"Daisy Duck shall play Juliet to my Romeo!" Paul Poser said. He turned to Mrs. Drake. "I positively *insist* on it."

Daisy's head swam. This was all going

terribly wrong! She wasn't an actor, she was an athlete! She'd rather watch a baseball game (or a rock concert) than a play. And now she was supposed to be in one?

"But I didn't even audition," Daisy said.

"Your audition was on the *stage of life*," Paul said. He waved his hands dramatically. "**And you aced it.**"

"That's a load of pigeon feathers," Daisy said. "I'm just here for Minnie. I mean, take a look at this dress she made! She even *looks* like a princess."

"Yes, yes, very impressive," Paul muttered. "But it matters not. You are Juliet. We will start rehearsals tomorrow."

"You sewed this dress yourself?" Mrs. Drake said to Minnie.

Minnie nodded.

"It's very fine work, Minnie. This is exactly the kind of dress I want to see onstage. Juliet will need a dress, and so will her nurse. And breeches

for the gentlemen . . . *so many breeches*!"

Daisy glanced at Minnie. She had a feeling she knew where this was going.

"Minnie, you simply must be the costume designer for the play!" Mrs. Drake declared.

"**And that is that!**"

Chapter 9

Minnie felt like crying. She had worked so hard on her audition! And now Paul Poser only had eyes for *Daisy*. Minnie was going to be a behind-the-scenes *tailor* while Daisy got all the glory. *She* would be sewing while Daisy was kissing Paul.

"Why me?" Minnie moaned. She wouldn't get to wear the dress she had spent hours making. Paul Poser was never going to ask her out. And it was all because of Daisy.

Worst. Day. Ever.

**"I won't wear something
Minnie makes,"** said a sneering voice.
Minnie looked up to see Abigail glaring at her.

"Yeah!" said Molly. Or maybe it was Millie.
Minnie could never tell them apart.

"I'd rather die than wear a costume she made,"
Abigail said to her groupies.

"Then get out of the play,"
Minnie heard herself say, "or *drop dead*."

Minnie gasped and clapped her hands over
her mouth. She was *never* this mean! But she was
just so upset . . .

"Hey! Let go of my arm!"

Minnie turned around, forgetting all about Abigail. Paul was dragging Daisy onto the stage.

"Hasten, fair Juliet!" Paul said to Daisy. "You have much to learn!"

"The name is *Daisy*," Daisy said. "Not Juliet. And I hate to break it to you, Paul, but you're not actually Romeo."

Paul sniffed. He handed Daisy a copy of the play. "I have an excellent eye for talent, you know," he said. "You have a natural gift for acting. Don't waste it."

Minnie's heart sank. Daisy looked as though she was really considering it. No! thought Minnie.

Don't do it, Daisy!

When you're BFFs with someone, you get to know them really well. Minnie knew what Daisy's favorite flavor of ice cream was (chocolate chunk) and what she was most proud of (winning the soccer tournament last year). She knew about Daisy's secret hopes (to sing in a rock band) and fears (clowns). Minnie almost always knew what Daisy was thinking.

And right now, Minnie knew that Daisy was thinking about taking the part. *I like playing sports in front of crowds,* Daisy was probably saying to herself. *That isn't very different from starring in a play. . . .*

Minnie sighed. Maybe if she came right out and asked Daisy not to take the part, she might still have a chance.

Daisy was her BFF, after all.

But when she went to find Daisy, suddenly Paul was there.

"What are you still doing here?" Paul said. "Begone, *costume designer*, we actors are *plying our craft*."

"Look," Minnie said hotly. Paul might be cute, but right now he was acting like a jerk. "I know every line in this play! How dare you—"

"Hist!" Paul said. **"Off with you."** And he turned his back.

Minnie had had all she could take. She gathered her dignity and walked out.

Chapter 10

CAST LIST

PAUL POSER AS ROMEO

DAISY DUCK AS JULIET

aisy looked around for Minnie. But when Daisy spotted her friend, she was walking out of the auditorium. She hadn't even stopped to congratulate Daisy on being offered the part of Juliet.

But Minnie probably had a lot of work to do, now that she was the costume designer for the whole play. And if Minnie was the costume designer, then that meant there wasn't any reason for Daisy not to take the part.

"What the heck," Daisy said. She

walked over to Paul Poser. "Okay, Paul," she said, "I'll play Juliet."

Rehearsals started the very next day. When Daisy arrived in the auditorium, she found Minnie waiting for her with a pink dress and a blond wig.

"I made your dress first, Daisy," Minnie said. She handed the dress to Daisy and then walked off without another word.

That's strange, Daisy thought. I guess she really is busy.

"We'll start with the balcony scene," Mrs. Drake announced. Daisy hurried backstage to change into her dress and put on her wig. But when she came out onto the balcony, Paul was already there.

"Aren't you supposed to be down on the ground?" Daisy said.

"Carry on, sweet Juliet," Paul replied. "I have a different staging in mind."

"Okay," Daisy said. **"O Romeo, Romeo!"** she began to recite.

"Cut!" Mrs. Drake cried from the stage below. "Paul, why are you up there? The script calls for you to be down *below* the balcony.

"Ods bodkins!" Paul cried. "It is vital that my importance be clear to the audience! Would they take note of a lowly peon below the balcony? I think not!"

Mrs. Drake looked tired. She must deal with this in every play, Daisy realized. Because Paul is in every play. Poor Mrs. Drake.

"Well," Mrs. Drake said with a sigh, "since you're already both up there, let's skip to the farewell scene in Act Three."

"I believe she means the kissing scene," Paul said. He nudged Daisy and winked at her.

"Oh, boy," Daisy muttered under her breath. So far she was actually enjoying herself. This play wasn't so bad! But she didn't like the idea of having to kiss Paul. **The only thing worse was having to kiss him in** **every** **rehearsal!**

Chapter 11

Down at the foot of the stage, Minnie was watching everything.

And she wasn't happy.

She didn't *blame* Daisy for taking the part. Not exactly. But Daisy hadn't even asked her! It was so typical. **Daisy was always the one in the spotlight.**

And now Daisy was going to kiss Paul. Paul was *Minnie's* crush! What if Paul kissed Daisy, and they fell in love? It was too awful to even think about.

Minnie had to stop them. For once in her life she was going to stand up for herself.

Up on the stage, Paul struck a very handsome pose. Daisy didn't look all that impressed. But the fact that Daisy could resist Paul didn't make Minnie feel better. **Once he kissed her, it would all be over.**

Minnie got up and hurried backstage.

Meanwhile, on the balcony, Paul was moving in for the kiss. He closed his eyes and leaned in toward Daisy.

"Yeah, I don't think so," Daisy said. She pulled back.

"'Farewell, farewell! One kiss and I'll descend—'" Paul started to say, when . . .

 The lights went out!

"Gadzooks!" Paul cried.

"Thank my lucky starlings," Daisy said. "Saved by a blackout!"

"Well, so much for today's rehearsal," Mrs. Drake said. "I can't direct a play I can't see. We might as well call it a day."

Paul heaved a disappointed sigh. Daisy heaved a relieved sigh. And backstage, Minnie sighed, too. But nobody heard her.

Chapter 12

Daisy's first day of rehearsals had been pretty strange. First Paul had been a complete diva, then there was that surprise blackout.

Good timing on the lights, Daisy thought as she walked home. They went out just as Paul was about to plant a big, wet kiss on my face. I wonder if Minnie was there? She would have liked to see that, I bet.

Daisy stopped short. "Minnie!" she said out loud.

Hurrying home, Daisy couldn't stop muttering, "Minnie, Minnie, Minnie!" under her breath. Finally, she was alone in her room.

"Minnie caused the blackout!" she yelled.

Usually, Daisy was the one who got mad and did crazy things like turning off the electricity. Minnie was supposed to be the calm one.

But Daisy knew how much Minnie liked Paul. She knew how much Minnie wanted to go out with him.

And Daisy had completely ruined that by taking the part of Juliet. No wonder Minnie was mad.

Maybe I shouldn't have taken the role of Juliet, Daisy thought.

"I don't even like theater!" She had slept through every class play she'd ever seen. Minnie had always been the one who loved watching things happen onstage.

But being onstage was different from being in the audience. Today's rehearsal had been a fiasco,

but Daisy had still enjoyed it. She liked having the warm spotlight shining on her, making her feel like she was up on a cloud.

But Minnie wasn't happy, and that meant Daisy wasn't happy. It wouldn't be any fun being in the play—not if she couldn't laugh with Minnie about it.

"I hate it when we fight," Daisy said. It didn't happen often. But when it did, it was always awful. And it was usually Daisy's fault.

Daisy was going to have to make things right. The next day, Daisy wrote a note to Minnie.

Minnie, are you mad at me? I'm sorry! Let's talk after class? I'll meet you at our usual table in the diner. BE THERE!

She tried to pass it to Minnie during social studies. But Minnie didn't notice her. She tried to pass it to Minnie during art, and Minnie stuck out her tongue at Daisy!

That was the last straw.

Daisy crumpled up the note and threw it as hard as she could. It hit Minnie right in the head.

"**Ouch!**" Minnie said. She rubbed her head.

"Read that note!" Daisy hissed at Minnie.

Minnie glared at her. But Daisy was glad to see Minnie bend down and pick up the note. She read it, and looked up at Daisy.

"Okay," Minnie said.

Chapter 13

"**A**ll right, Minnie," Daisy said as she sat down at their usual booth in the diner. "I'm sorry."

"Sure," Minnie said. She played with her ice cream. She didn't look at Daisy.

"I'm *sorry*," Daisy said. Minnie still didn't look up. "Look, would you *just* talk to me, please?"

"Sure," Minnie said. She glared at Daisy. "How is the play going? Are you having fun with Paul? You guys must be pretty close by now."

Ew. Daisy would rather get close to an anteater than Paul. An anteater with bad breath.

"Not really," Daisy said. "But I know that's why you're mad—"

"I *am* mad!" Minnie said. **"I'm really mad at you!** And I **hate** being mad at you!" She looked more sad than angry.

"You're my best friend," Minnie said. Her voice was soft. "But you betrayed me, Daisy."

Here we are, Daisy thought. This is the heart of it.

"You knew I wanted to be Juliet," Minnie said. "You *knew* it, and you took the part. Without even asking me!" Minnie sniffled. "I worked so hard on that audition. And I never even got to try out."

"Minnie . . ." Daisy said. "Yes, I should have asked you. But did you really want the part?"

"Yes!" Minnie said.

"Or did you just want a chance to kiss Paul Poser?" Daisy finished.

"Well . . ." Minnie said. She thought it over. She sighed. "You have a point," Minnie said. "But acting in a play with

him was my only chance. Now he's never going to think I'm special. Or interesting. Or pretty."

"But you *are* special and interesting and pretty," Daisy said. Minnie smiled a little. Daisy went on, **"Only a complete jerk wouldn't notice you."**

"Paul isn't a complete jerk," Minnie said. "Well, he *did* tell me to 'begone.'"

Daisy rolled her eyes.

"But he just wanted to focus on his acting!" Minnie said. "He's an *artist*, Daisy."

"Artist or not," Daisy said, "he's still a boy. If he likes you, you'll know."

"And if he doesn't?" Minnie asked, looking worried.

"Then he's got terrible taste," Daisy said. Minnie hugged her.

Daisy breathed a big sigh of relief. **They were BFFs again.**

Chapter 14

"'Hey nonny, nonny,'" Minnie sang. She was working on Lady Capulet's gown.

"'Sigh no more, ladies, sigh no'—nuts!" Minnie pricked her finger and jumped—and accidentally yanked at the dress's seam.

Minnie sighed. She ripped the uneven stitches out and started sewing again. Making costumes for the entire cast was a big job. But she was surprised to find herself having fun. Lady Capulet's gown was going to be beautiful. **Minnie was proud of her work.**

I'm good at this, Minnie thought as she folded the finished dress. Honestly, I'm probably better at this than I would be at acting. And people had complimented her. Just the other day, Leonard had told Minnie he loved his costume.

Maybe Paul Poser would notice her after all.
Maybe she'd still get that kiss.
Minnie began to daydream:

Paul hurried through the halls of Mouston Central School. "Whither, oh, whither is Minnie?" he said. Then he saw her. She was bent over a dress—a beautiful, frilly cupcake of a dress. She was sewing on the last ruffle.

"Minnie, you make the most wonderful clothes," Paul said. **"I love to watch you sew."**

Minnie blushed. "Oh, it's nothing, Paul," she said.

"No, you are amazing!" Paul took her hand. "Minnie," he said shyly, "Will you . . . would you . . . Could you go to the movies with me?"

Minnie smiled. She knew just how it was going to go. She and Paul would watch a movie. Then Paul would take Minnie out for an ice-cream sundae. The next

weekend, they'd do it all again. They would be sweethearts for years! They'd even go to the same college! After graduation, Paul would get down on one knee.

"Minnie," he'd say, **"I've always loved you. Will you marry me?"**

They would get married on a beach, with Daisy as the maid of honor! Paul and Minnie Poser would have two children, a boy and a girl.

It was all going to work out perfectly . . . because Minnie was going to make the handsomest costume for Paul. And he would finally notice her!

Chapter 15

"**S**ewing kit? Check. Extra fabric? Check. Buttons? Check. Pattern book? Check. Checklist? Check!"

Minnie hurried backstage. It was time to do the costume fittings for the show.

"Leonard, you're first!" she called. Leonard arrived, holding up his pants with one hand.

"Breeches too loose?" Minnie asked. She grabbed her pincushion and a piece of chalk and went to work. In no time, Leonard was walking off in pants that fit perfectly.

"Next!" Minnie called. She was on fire! Maybe Paul would notice how busy she was.

And she really was busy! People kept losing buttons or changing their minds about how long their skirts should be. Abigail and her two little pals were the worst.

"Minnie, I hate my sleeves!"

"Minnie, this cap doesn't fit!"

"Minnie, where are my shoes?"

Minnie was sure they were annoying her on purpose. As soon as she turned her back, one of them would burst a seam.

RRRIP!

It was a tiring day. At the end of rehearsal, Minnie was ready to fall down. She had hemmed seven dresses, tailored six pairs of pants, and shined more shoes than she could count.

But Minnie was happy.

"Ahem," said a shy voice behind her. Minnie turned. It was Paul!

"Say, ah, Minnie," Paul said. He trailed off and looked at the floor. He looked . . . bashful!

"Yes, Paul?" Minnie said. This was it! He looked so shy . . . so embarrassed . . . he was *definitely* about to ask her out!

"Well, I, that is . . ." Paul stuttered. "I just wanted to ask you . . . if you would . . .

"Would you replace the buttons on my breeches?" Paul said.

Minnie gaped at him.

"It's just that they're yellow," Paul said. "And they clash with my perfectly white teeth!"

"Oh," Minnie said. "Yes. Of course." Her

heart sank. Was that all she was to Paul? A tailor?

"I knew I could count on you," Paul said. He tossed the pants at Minnie. She caught them before they hit her in the face.

"I'll need those tomorrow, obviously," Paul said.

"**Obviously,**" Minnie echoed.

"Well, I'll see ya!" Paul said. He turned and waved. "I'm off to practice writing my autograph! After this play, **I'll be an even bigger star than I already am!**"

Minnie watched him go. She sighed. She had really thought Paul was going to ask her out. But he hadn't.

Maybe if Minnie did a really great job with the new buttons, he would finally notice her. But she was beginning to think it might be a lost cause.

"**You get one more chance, Paul Poser**," Minnie said to herself. "And then **I'm giving up on you.**"

Chapter 16

At the next rehearsal, Minnie was on high alert! She eyed Paul while she sewed new buttons onto his breeches. She watched him while she laced up Millie's corset. She listened for his voice while she adjusted Leonard's cap.

Paul spent a lot of time looking at himself in the mirror. He kept fiddling with his hairdo.

Minnie was beginning to wonder if Daisy was right. **Was Paul only interested in Paul?**

Minnie tried to keep a tally of Paul's behavior.

But she kept getting distracted . . . **by Daisy!**

"'My only love sprung from my only hate!'"
Daisy cried from the stage. "'Too early seen
unknown, and known too late!'"

A shiver ran down Minnie's spine. Daisy was
really good! She walked across the stage as if she
owned it. She was radiant in the gown Minnie
had made for her. She knew all her lines. And she
really made Minnie believe that she was **Juliet!**

"Wow," Millie said. Or maybe it was Molly. Minnie always forgot. **"Daisy is really good!"**

"Shut it, Molly," Abigail said.

"Yes, please do," Paul agreed. "Daisy is getting too big for her britches," Paul said sourly. "Soon she's going to start thinking she's as good as me."

"Nobody's as good as you, Paul," Molly said. She fluttered her eyelashes at him.

Minnie rolled her eyes. Was that what she was like around Paul? She felt a little embarrassed. But then Paul whipped around to glare at Molly.

"Who cares what you think, Millie?" Paul snapped.

"Um, I'm Molly," she replied. Molly looked like she was about to cry.

"Millie, Molly, whatever. Nobody cares what you think," Paul said. "You're a nobody. Don't talk to me." He stomped off in a huff.

Molly ran off in the opposite direction, crying.

Minnie was shocked. **What a jerk!** Paul couldn't stand to see Daisy having her moment in the spotlight. So he took it out on poor Molly!

That was enough. What had she seen in Paul? She couldn't even remember! Well, he *was* very handsome. But he was also a terrible person!

"You had a second chance, buddy," Minnie said to Paul. She poked him in the chest. He looked confused. "And you blew it."

Chapter 17

"You were great in rehearsal today, Daisy,"
Minnie said later that night. They were
catching up on the phone.

"Aw, thanks, Min," Daisy said. "That means a
lot, coming from you. How's your job going?"

"I've got my hands full!" Minnie said. "But I'm
really enjoying it!"

"Don't forget you're my understudy, too!" Daisy
reminded her. "If I lose my voice from yelling at
Paul, you'll have to take over."

"Oh, boy," Minnie said. "So, speaking of Paul ..."

"Uh-oh," Daisy said. "What does *that* mean?"

"Daisy, you were right about him all along! He was so jealous about how good you were today that he said something really mean to Molly! He made her cry!"

"**Yikes,**" Daisy said. "They should call him **Paul Loser** instead of Paul Poser."

"I had no idea he was so selfish," Minnie said. "He's *awful*."

"You were blinded by his big brown eyes and

his awesome hair," Daisy said. "It happens to the best of us. But I'm so glad you hate him now. It means I can complain about him all I want!"

Minnie laughed. "Okay," she said. "Go right ahead."

"He did the whole 'Juliet is the sun' speech looking into a *mirror*," Daisy said.

Minnie giggled. "We should call the play *Romeo and Romeo (And Juliet, Too, I Guess)*. That's what he thinks it is!"

Chapter 18

The days and weeks went by. The tech kids built a set for the play. Everyone finally learned all their lines—even Leonard.

Once Minnie was finished making the costumes, she didn't have much to do. She was Daisy's understudy, but she already knew the lines. And it wasn't as though Daisy would ever miss the night of a performance.

So Minnie spent a lot of time in the back of the auditorium, watching the actors rehearse. She was getting a little bored, to tell the truth.

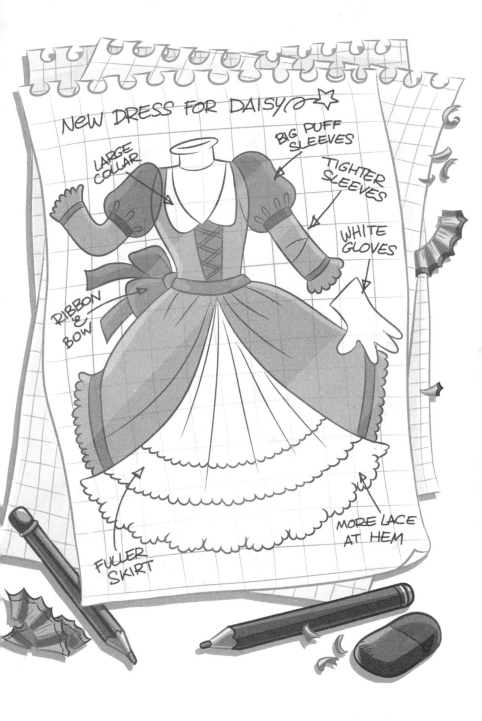

"I never thought I'd miss sewing," Minnie muttered. She watched Daisy onstage, swishing back and forth in her pretty pink dress.

"I wish that dress swished better," Minnie said to herself. "Maybe if I added another petticoat? But then I'd have to recut the skirt. And lengthen the hem. Hmm."

Minnie started scribbling.

"Minnie? Rehearsal is over. Minnie? *Minnie!*"

Minnie looked up, startled. Daisy was standing right in front of her. She tweaked Minnie's bow. "What are you working so hard on?"

"I want to make you a new dress," Minnie said. "I don't like how this one swishes."

"You're nuts," Daisy said. "Come on, forget about that for ten minutes. Let's go for a bike ride."

"There's no time for bike rides!" Minnie cried. She grabbed Daisy's hand. "Come with me! We're going to make you a new dress."

Back at Minnie's house, Daisy watched as her friend sewed up a storm.

"But Minnie," Daisy said, "I like my dress the way it is!"

"It just won't do, Daisy!" Minnie said. Minnie pulled the new dress from the sewing machine. "Here, try this one on."

Daisy modeled the new dress for Minnie. It was better . . . but it wasn't perfect. Minnie went back to work.

"Try it now," she said. "No, now it's too swishy. And I don't like the neckline."

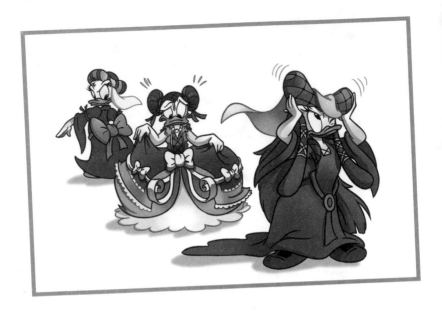

By the next morning, Minnie had altered the new dress seven more times.

"Try it now," Minnie said. Daisy moaned. She was lying facedown on Minnie's bed. "Come on, Daisy," Minnie crooned. "Just one more time. I promise!"

Daisy tottered to her feet. She put on the dress (which looked almost exactly like the *original* dress Minnie had made). "Oh, *perfect!*" Minnie said. "Now you're *really* Juliet!"

"Forsooth, thou art a crazy person," Daisy said.

efore Minnie knew it, the big night had arrived. There were just a few hours left before the performance.

"Minnie, I'm so nervous!" Daisy said. "Come for a bike ride with me. I need to get some air."

"I don't know, Daisy," Minnie said. "I've got an awful lot of last-minute work to do for tonight. Like making sure Paul's buttons match his teeth . . ."

Daisy laughed, but she was so nervous it came out as a quack.

"Fine, you win," Minnie said.

The two friends coasted along the beach.

"Why are you wearing your costume already?" Minnie said.

BFF

"I am in *character*, milady," Daisy said. "It is what we actors do before a play. Please, call me Juliet."

"Okay, Juliet," Minnie said. "But did they really have bicycles in Shakespeare's time?"

"It matters not," Daisy said.

MiNNiE

DAISY

"I just worry that your dress might get caught in the—"

Rrrrip!

"Alack! Fie! A pox on this bicycle!" Daisy cried. Her long pink skirt had gotten tangled in one of the bicycle's tires. A big chunk of the petticoat and some of the skirt had torn off.

"Oh, dear," Minnie said. This was bad.

"Minnie, the play doth begin anon! Whatever shall I do? Thou must remedy it!" Daisy said. She wrung her hands at Minnie.

"I think you'd better snap out of character," Minnie said. "I can't actually talk to you as Juliet."

"Minnie!" Daisy wailed, dropping the accent. "My pretty dress is ruined!"

Chapter 20

"**I** can't go onstage like this!" Daisy cried. "What am I going to *do*?"

"**Calm down!**" Minnie said. "We're going to figure this out."

"Sew it back on!" Daisy said. "Fix it, Minnie!"

"I can't," Minnie said. "There's no time. I have so much to do backstage. But don't you still have your original costume? The one that wasn't swishy enough?"

"Yes!" Daisy said. She brightened up. "It swished fine. You were just bored."

"So go get it," Minnie said. "It's probably in your closet, right?"

"I think? I don't remember! Argh!" Daisy tore at her wig. "Come with me, Minnie. Help me find it!"

"Daisy, I *can't*," Minnie said again. "I have to be backstage in ten minutes. Paul will completely freak out if his buttons aren't just right."

Daisy hopped onto her bike and tore off. She rode faster than she ever had before. She had no time to spare. Her house was pretty far from the school, and the play was starting—Daisy checked her watch— **really soon!**

When she got to her house, Daisy ditched her bike on the sidewalk and ran inside. She quickly changed into regular clothes. No way was she riding in her backup dress! She grabbed the dress from her closet and ran back to her bike.

"Romeo, I'm on my way!" she yelled, and pedaled as hard as she could.

I can't BELIEVE IT!!

hat a disaster! The play was supposed to start any minute . . . and Daisy was just getting to the school! If only Minnie had been able to sew up her dress when it ripped.

But the show couldn't go on without Juliet, right?

Wait a minute.

Minnie was Daisy's understudy.

Daisy saw red.

Minnie wants to play Juliet! Daisy thought. She's always wanted to play Juliet! I should have figured it out when she mentioned Paul's buttons. She isn't over him! This is her chance to get me out of the spotlight . . . and kiss Paul!

Minnie was going to get all the glory! Now Daisy would *never* be a famous actress. She'd never win a *Mouscar* award.

"How could Minnie do this to me!?" Daisy said as she ran through the halls of the school.

"No more Ms. Nice Duck," Daisy said. She was nearly at the backstage door. And she was

fuming.

"I'm going to do whatever it takes. **I'll stop the show!** I will not let Minnie steal my role!"

In the back of her head, a tiny little voice reminded Daisy not to jump to conclusions. But Daisy squashed the little voice and darted into the maze of scenery and actors backstage.

"Oh Juuuuliet!" Daisy heard Minnie's voice. It was coming from onstage. "There's a young man named Romeo here to seeee you!"

Daisy peered out from the wings. Onstage, Minnie was **wearing her princess dress.** She was hanging over the balcony. The people in the audience were all muttering. They looked confused.

"This part isn't in the play, is it?" Minnie heard one of the audience members say.

Daisy let out a big breath. **Minnie wasn't trying to steal her part.** She was making up lines to keep the play going until Daisy could arrive!

Daisy had been so, so wrong about her friend.

"Hurry, Daisy!" whispered Leonard. "She's been up there for ten minutes! You gotta get onstage before she runs out of stuff to say!"

SWeeT!

Daisy changed into her costume as fast as she could.

"Wheeeere could Juliet beeee?" Minnie yelled from the balcony.

Daisy ran up the backstage stairs toward the balcony.

"Lo, here I am!" Daisy called out. Minnie spun around and grinned at her.

"Thanks for saving my tail feather, BFF," Daisy whispered to Minnie. **"You're the best."**

innie hurried off the balcony, and Daisy took her place. Now was her moment. The play could go on!

"'O Romeo, Romeo,'" Daisy sang out. "'Wherefore art thou Romeo?'"

There was an awkward pause. Daisy looked down at the stage. Paul Poser was there in his Romeo costume, and he looked really, really mad.

Uh-oh.

"I thank thee for joining us, at long last," Paul said sarcastically. "I hope thou didst not hurry. I

hmmm...

was only waiting here for eons and eons and eons."

"I'm sure that part isn't in the original!" someone in the audience whispered.

Daisy was going to have to fix this, and fast. It was a good thing she knew how to cheer up Paul Poser.

"Romeo, thou art the moon and the stars," she said. "*And* thou art **very nice** to have waited for me."

Paul scowled.

"And thy buttons do complement thy bright, shiny teeth," Daisy added. Paul looked a little less mad.

"And thy hair is awesome," Daisy said. "Thou lookest totally dreamy."

"Did she say 'dreamy'?" someone in the audience whispered.

"Did she say 'awesome'?" someone else said.

Onstage, Daisy was looking at Paul, and she could tell her compliments had worked—even if Shakespeare hadn't written them.

"I thank thee, my lady," Paul said. He bowed

deeply and swished his hat to the side. "Thou art too kind. It is true, my hair is verily very dashing."

"And?" Daisy said, prompting him. She smiled encouragingly.

"And . . . 'with love's light wings did I oe'r-perch these walls,'" Paul said, getting back into character. "'For stony limits cannot hold love out.'"

Daisy smiled. They were back in business.

"'Oh, gentle Romeo,'" she said, "'if thou dost love, pronounce it faithfully.'"

Chapter 23

An hour and a half later . . .

"'For never was a story of more woe,'"
Leonard said solemnly, "'than this of Juliet and
her Romeo.'"

The curtain went down. The play was over.

There was a hushed pause. **And then
the audience leaped to their
feet, clapping!**

Daisy and Paul hurried out to take their bows.
Daisy grabbed Minnie's hand and tugged her
onstage with them. "You saved the day," Daisy

said to Minnie, "so you should get some glory, too!"

Minnie bowed with Daisy and Paul. She and Daisy couldn't stop grinning at each other!

After the curtain went down for the final time, **Daisy gave Minnie a big hug.**

"Minnie, I have to confess something," Daisy said. She hung her head. "I thought you

wanted to steal my role. But the second I got here I realized I was wrong. I never should have doubted you! You're always there for me."

"What are BFFs for?" Minnie said. Daisy hugged her again.

"Are you sad it's all over?" Minnie asked Daisy.

"A little bit," Daisy said. "Being Juliet was pretty amazing. I never knew I could act, you know? But I won't miss having to put up with Paul in rehearsal all the time."

Minnie winced. She felt a little embarrassed about her old crush on Paul.

"You're completely over him, right?" Daisy said. "Because he doesn't deserve you."

"**I am over him,**" Minnie said. "In fact, I left him a little souvenir to remember me by."

"Uh-oh," Daisy said. "Minnie, **what did you do?**"

innie and Daisy changed out of their costumes. They were just going to celebrate, when . . .

"Augh!"

Paul Poser came running up to Minnie.

"My buttons are covered in glue!" he said. "Minnie, I can't get out of my costume because my hands are stuck to it!"

"That's terrible," Minnie said with a completely straight face. "Isn't that terrible, Daisy?"

"Yes," Daisy said. She was trying not to laugh. "Terrible."

"Well, good luck with that!" Minnie waved at Paul. "We've got to be going now."

"**Wait!**" Paul said. "**Halt! Stop! I command you!**"

"You command me?" Minnie said.

"You are the costume designer!" Paul said. He tried to point at Minnie, but his hand was stuck to his jacket. "Fix this!"

"**Fix it?** Like how I made your buttons match your teeth?" Minnie asked.

"Yes!"

"Like how I created the perfect costume for you to play the perfect Romeo?"

"Yes!"

"You really were wonderful," Minnie said.

"I know," Paul said. "Now can you—?"

"Staying in character is very important to actors, isn't it, Daisy?" Minnie winked at her friend.

"Very," Daisy agreed.

"So what's the problem?" Minnie said to Paul. "You love staying in character, so just stay in your costume!"

And she walked off arm in arm with Daisy, giggling.